Bolton
Council

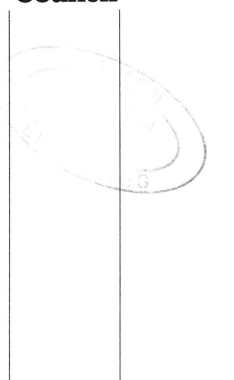

Please return/ renew this item
by the last date shown.
Books can also be renewed at
www.bolton.gov.uk/libra

Chapter 1

Long ago, in Japan, there lived an old woman.

Every day, she washed clothes in the river.

And every day, she wished that she had a child

to love, for she had always longed for a child.

One day, the old woman saw a huge peach

floating by on the water.

She scooped it up and rolled it home.

"Now I will have a feast for supper," she thought.

But when she cut the peach open she found,

not a stone, but a tiny baby boy.

The woman picked him up and cuddled him.

"You're my little peach boy," she said.

"I'll call you Momotaro, which means just that.

And I will be your mother."

3

Momotaro the Peach Boy grew up
healthy and happy. His mother fed him
all the good things she could afford.
But what Momotaro liked best were
the cakes she made from the millet
and rice which she grew in the fields.

"Just one of these cakes will give you
the strength of ten men," she told him.
After Momotaro ate one, he would flex his arms,
pick his mother up and swing her round.

Chapter 2

One day, three ogres came to live on an island

on the river. They were terrible bullies

who had been stealing treasure from villages

and towns all over Japan.

They built a big black fort on the island

in which to hide their stolen treasures.

6

There was a scarlet ogre
with bloodshot eyes,

a purple ogre with

a long tongue,

and a huge yellow ogre with

pointed gold teeth.

The ogres soon ate all the food on the island.
In the distance, they could see the village where
Momotaro and his mother lived. They could see
the fruit trees and the green fields.

One day, they decided to wade across the river. They picked all the fruit from the trees and they stole all the grain. They stole everything they could.

Before long, everyone in the village became thin and hungry. In Momotaro's house, his mother made her very last cakes. "There's no more grain," she said sadly. "What will we do?"

"These are your best cakes ever," said Momotaro, taking a bite. "I'm going to take them with me when I go to fight the ogres."

"But the ogres will kill you!" cried his mother.

"Not me," said Momotaro. "You said that one of these cakes will give me the strength of ten men."

His mother made him some armour.

"Momotaro, Little Peach Boy, you are Japan's strongest warrior!" she told him, proudly.

Then Momotaro set out, clutching a bag of his mother's cakes.

Chapter 3

At the end of the village, Momotaro met a dog.

"Momotaro, Little Peach Boy," it barked.

"Where are you going?"

"I'm going to the island," said Momotaro,

"to fight the ogres."

"If you give me one of your mother's cakes,"

barked the dog, "I'll come with you."

Momotaro smiled. "If you eat one, you'll be

as strong as ten men. My mother said so."

On his way to the river, Momotaro met a monkey.

"Please give me one of your mother's cakes,"

the monkey begged.

"Will you come with us to fight the ogres?"

asked Momotaro.

"Ha! An ogre will mean nothing to me!"

said the monkey. "I have heard that just one

of your mother's cakes will give me

the strength of ten men."

They arrived at the river. All the boats were moored along the shore. No fisherman had dared to go out fishing with the ogres nearby. Momotaro, the dog and the monkey climbed aboard a boat and set off.

Halfway to the island, a crane swooped down
on them. "Momotaro, Little Peach Boy!"
screeched the crane. "Where are you going?"
"To the island," said Momotaro, "to fight the ogres."
"Give me one of your mother's cakes,"
said the crane, "and I'll come with you."

17

When they reached the fort, the tall gates

were locked. Momotaro hammered on them.

"Who's making all that noise?"

roared the scarlet ogre.

"Momotaro, Japan's Strongest Warrior!"

Momotaro cried.

"Momotaro? A peach boy?"

sneered the scarlet ogre.

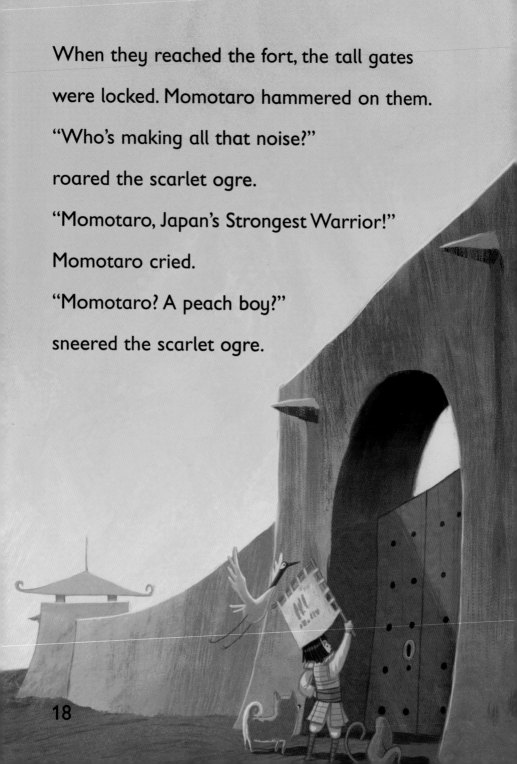

19

"I'll get the keys," screeched the crane.

She spread her huge wings and flew over the wall.

The heavy keys were hanging on a huge iron hook.

But after eating the cake, she could pick them up

as if they were twigs and drop them

at Momotaro's feet.

Momotaro turned the key and the gates
creaked open. There stood the scarlet ogre,
his crimson eyes blazing.

Momotaro waved his flag. "I'm Momotaro,
Japan's Strongest Warrior," he shouted.

"And I've come to fight you."

"You must be joking!" laughed the scarlet ogre.

"Look," he called to his brothers.

"Come and see what we have here!"

"Who is this little peach boy?"

sniggered the purple ogre.

The yellow ogre clashed his bright gold teeth.

"He's not very big," he dribbled, "but he'd make

a tasty snack."

The yellow ogre lunged at Momotaro,

but the dog bit his legs.

Then the monkey leapt on the yellow ogre's back

and thumped his shoulders.

The purple ogre curled his tongue around

Momotaro's neck, but the crane swooped down,

and pecked at his eyes.

"So you let your friends fight for you," sneered the scarlet ogre. "Can't you fight your own battles?"

But by then, Momotaro had eaten the rest of his mother's cakes ...

After many hours, the ogres had to give up.

"You're much too strong for us," they groaned.

"But please don't kill us."

"If you promise to go away," said Momotaro,

"and not trouble anyone any more,

then I will let you go unharmed."

"We promise," gasped the ogres,

and they vanished in a cloud of smoke.

Momotaro went to look for all the food

that the ogres had stolen

from his village.

Inside the fort, he found

the ogres' treasure.

They loaded it into the boat –

gold, silver, rubies

and diamonds.

Momotaro's village became rich.

Once again, the fishermen fished, and the peach

trees blossomed, and children went on picnics

to the island on the river.

The dog went to live with Momotaro

and his mother, and the monkey made his home

among the fruit trees in the orchard.

"I'm off!" screeched the crane. "But I'll be back

in the spring for more of your mother's cakes."

Momotaro became famous throughout Japan, and so did his mother's cakes. Even the emperor got to hear the story of Momotaro and the ogres. And when Momotaro grew up, he married one of the emperor's daughters – but that is another story.

Things to think about

1. Why is Momotaro's mother proud of him when he leaves to fight the ogres?
2. Do you think the name "Little Peach Boy" makes Momotaro seem like a fearsome warrior?
3. Can you think of two themes in this story?
4. Do you think Momotaro would have succeeded in beating the ogres if he had travelled alone?
5. Can you think of any other stories where the bravery of a small hero defeats the might of larger enemies?

Write it yourself

One of the themes in this story is bravery.
Now try to write your own story with a similar theme.
Plan your story before you begin to write it.
Start off with a story map:
• a beginning to introduce the characters and where and when your story is set (the setting);
• a problem which the main characters will need to fix in the story;
• an ending where the problems are resolved.

Get writing! Try to create interesting characters, not just by telling your reader what they are like, but showing this through how they say things. For example, you could use begged, shouted, sneered, sniggered.

Notes for parents and carers

Independent reading
The aim of independent reading is to read this book with ease. This series is designed to provide an opportunity for your child to read for pleasure and enjoyment. These notes are written for you to help your child make the most of this book.

About the book
This story is based on a traditional Japanese tale. There are many versions of it, and the name of Momotaro is famous throughout Japan. All versions agree that Momotaro looked after his parents, and that he was kind and brave for going on his journey to defeat the ogres.

Before reading
Ask your child why they have selected this book. Look at the title and blurb together. What do they think it will be about? Do they think they will like it?

During reading
Encourage your child to read independently. If they get stuck on a longer word, remind them that they can find syllable chunks that can be sounded out from left to right. They can also read on in the sentence and think about what would make sense.

After reading
Support comprehension by talking about the story. What happened?
Then help your child think about the messages in the book that go beyond the story, using the questions on the page opposite. Give your child a chance to respond to the story, asking:
Did you enjoy the story and why? Who was your favourite character?
What was your favourite part? What did you expect to happen at the end?

Franklin Watts
First published in Great Britain in 2018
by The Watts Publishing Group

Series Editors: Jackie Hamley and Melanie Palmer
Series Advisors: Dr Sue Bodman and Glen Franklin
Series Designer: Peter Scoulding

A CIP catalogue record for this book is
available from the British Library.

ISBN 978 1 4451 6245 4 (hbk)
ISBN 978 1 4451 6313 0 (pbk)
ISBN 978 1 4451 6314 7 (library ebook)

Printed in China

Franklin Watts
An imprint of
Hachette Children's Group
Part of The Watts Publishing Group
Carmelite House
50 Victoria Embankment
London EC4Y 0DZ

An Hachette UK Company
www.hachette.co.uk

www.franklinwatts.co.uk

FSC
www.fsc.org
MIX
Paper from
responsible sources
FSC® C104740